A MEDAL FOR
LEROY

michael morpurgo

A MEDAL FOR LEROY

Illustrated by Michael Foreman

HarperCollins *Children's Books*

First published in hardback and paperback in Great Britain by
HarperCollins *Children's Books* in 2012
This edition published in 2013
HarperCollins *Children's Books* is a division of HarperCollins*Publishers* Ltd,
1 London Bridge Street, London SE1 9GF

For videos, audio, interviews and more, visit www.michaelmorpurgo.com

The HarperCollins website address is: www.harpercollins.co.uk

1

Text copyright © Michael Morpurgo 2012
Illustrations copyright © Michael Foreman 2012
© WireImage/Getty Images (Lance Corporal Johnson Beharry)
© Lordprice Collection/Alamy (Play the Greater Game poster)
© Image Courtesy of The Advertising Archives (Red Cross poster)
Photograph (Walter Tull) by kind permission of Pat Justad

ISBN 978-0-00-796699-8

Michael Morpurgo and Michael Foreman assert the moral right to be identified
as the author and illustrator of the work.

Printed and bound CPI Group (UK) Ltd, Croydon, CR0 4YY

MIX
Paper from
responsible sources
FSC
www.fsc.org   FSC™ C007454

FSC™ is a non-profit international organisation established to promote
the responsible management of the world's forests. Products carrying the
FSC label are independently certified to assure consumers that they come
from forests that are managed to meet the social, economic and
ecological needs of present and future generations,
and other controlled sources.

Find out more about HarperCollins and the environment at
www.harpercollins.co.uk/green

To Lieutenant Walter Tull
1888–1918

March 2, 2012

When it came to it, I wasn't entirely sure what we were doing walking up that hillside in Belgium. Christine's hand came into mine as we walked. Were we burying the past, righting a wrong, or simply paying our respects? Were we doing it for ourselves, or was it for Maman and Papa, or Auntie Snowdrop and Auntie Pish, or Grandfather Leroy?

It had happened somewhere in this field, definitely this field – we knew that much from the maps. We knew Leroy had run on ahead of the others, that he was leading the attack. But where exactly had it happened? Closer to the crest of the hill, near the trees? Probably. Nearer the farm buildings? Maybe. We had so little to go on.

Jasper had run on ahead of us, and was snuffling about under a fallen tree at the edge of the wood. Then he was exploring along the tree line on the crest of the hill, nose to the ground.

"Wherever Jasper stops," I said, "if he ever does, wherever he next sits down for a rest, that's where we'll do it. Agreed?"

Poodle

I GREW UP IN THE 1940S IN LONDON, JUST AFTER
the war. When I was a boy, my friends called
me 'Poodle'. I didn't mind that much. I'd have
preferred they called me Michael – it was my
real name after all – but they rarely did.

I didn't have a father, not one that I ever knew anyway. You don't miss what you've never had, so I didn't mind that either, not much. There were compensations too. Not having a father made me different. Most of my pals at school lived in two-parent families – a few had three or even four parents, if you count step-families. I had just the one parent, Maman, and no brothers and sisters either. That made me special. I liked being different. I liked feeling special.

Maman was French, and spoke English as if it was French, with lots of hand-waving, conducting her words with her hands, her voice as full of expression as her eyes. We spoke mostly French at home – she insisted on it, so that I could grow up 'dreaming in both languages' as she put it, which I could and still do; but that was why her English accent never improved. At the school gates when she sometimes came to fetch me I'd feel proud of her Frenchness. With her short dark hair and olive brown skin, and her accent, she neither looked nor sounded like the other mothers. We had a book at school on great heroes and heroines, and Maman looked just like Joan of Arc in that book, only a bit older.

But being half French had its difficulties. I was 'Poodle' on account of my frizzy black hair, and because I was a bit French. Poodles are known in England as a very French kind of dog, so Maman told me. Even she would call me 'my little poodle' sometimes, which I have to say I preferred to *'mon petit chou'* –

my little cabbage, her favourite name for me. At school I had all sorts of other playground nicknames besides 'Poodle'. 'Froggie' was one, because in those days French people were often called 'Frogs'. I didn't much like that. Maman told me not to worry. "It's because they think we all eat nothing but frogs' legs. Just call them 'Roast beef' back," Maman told me. "That's what we French call the English."

So I tried it. They just thought it was funny and laughed. So from then on it became a sort of joke around the school – we'd even have pick-up football teams in the playground called the Roastbeefs and the Froggies. In the end I was English enough to be acceptable to them, and to feel one of them. Maybe that was why I never much minded what they called me – it was all done in fun, most of the time, anyway.

Somehow it had got around the school, and all down the street, about my father – I don't know how, because I never said anything. Everyone seemed to know why Maman was always alone – and not just at the school gates, but at Nativity plays at Christmas time, at football matches. It was common knowledge that my father had been killed in the war. Whenever the war was spoken of around me – and it was spoken of often when I was growing up – voices would drop to a respectful, almost reverential whisper, and people would look at me sideways, admiringly, sympathetically, enviously even. I didn't know much more about my father than they did. But I liked the admiration and the sympathy, and the envy too.

All Maman had told me was that my father was called Roy, that he had been in the RAF, a Spitfire pilot, a Flight Lieutenant, and that he had been shot down over the English Channel in the summer of 1940. They had only been married for six months – six months, two weeks and one day – she was always very precise about it when I asked about Papa. He'd been adopted as a baby by his aunties, after their sister, his mother, had been killed in a Zeppelin raid on London. So he'd grown up with his aunties by the sea in Folkestone in Kent, and gone to school there. He was twenty-one when he died, she said.

That's just about all I knew, all she would tell me anyway. No matter how much I asked, and I did, and more often as I grew up, she would say little more about him. I know now how painful it must have been for her to talk of him, but at the time I remember feeling very upset, angry almost towards her. He was my father, wasn't he? It felt to me as if she was keeping him all for herself. Occasionally after a football match, or when I'd run down to the corner shop on an errand for old Ma Merritt who lived next door to us, Maman might say something like: "Your Papa would have been so proud of you. I so wish he'd known you." But never anything more, nothing about him, nothing that helped me to imagine what sort of a man he might have been.

Sometimes, on the anniversary of his death or on Remembrance Day perhaps, she'd become tearful, and bring out her photograph album to show me. She couldn't speak as she turned the pages and I knew better than to ask any more of my questions. It was as I gazed at him in those photos, and as he looked back up at me, that I really missed knowing him. In truth, it was only ever a momentary pang, but each time I looked into his face, it set me wondering. I tried to feel sad about him but I found it hard. He was, in the end, and I knew it, just a face in a photo to me. I felt bad about it, bad about not feeling sad, I mean. If I cried with Maman – and I did sometimes over that album – I cried only because I could tell Maman was aching with grief inside.

Some nights when I was little, I'd hear Maman crying herself to sleep in her room. I used to go to her bed then and crawl in with her. She'd hold me tight and say nothing. Sometimes at moments like that I felt she really wanted to tell me more about him, and I longed to ask, but I knew that to ask would be to intrude on her grief and maybe make it worse for her. Time and again I'd let the moment pass. I'd try asking her another time, but whenever I did, she'd look away, clam up, or simply change the subject – she was very good at changing the subject. I didn't understand then that her loss was still too sharp, her memories too fresh, or that maybe she was just trying to keep her pain to herself,

to protect me perhaps, so as not to upset
me. I only knew that I wanted to know more
about him, and she wouldn't tell me.

Papa's Medal

AS TIME PASSED, SHE DID BEGIN TO SPEAK OF HIM a little more often and more freely too, but even then only in answer to my endless pestering. I remember we were moving house – just down the road, not far, from 83 to

24 Philbeach Gardens, near Earls Court in London – when the bottom fell out of the cardboard box I was carrying upstairs in our new house, spilling everything down the staircase. It was as I began to pick things up that I came across the medal, silver with a blue and white ribbon attached. I guessed it must have been Papa's, and asked Maman what he had won it for.

"For bravery," she told me. "Your Papa was very brave, you know. They were all brave, all those fighter pilots." Then she said, "It was his, so now it's yours. You can keep it if you like."

So that was why, from then on, I always kept Papa's silver medal on my mantelpiece alongside all my football cups and shields. I'd look at it often, touch it for luck sometimes when I was going off to play a football match, or before a spelling test at school. Occasionally, in the secrecy of my bedroom, I'd pin it on, look at myself in the mirror, and wonder if I could ever have been as brave as he was. I discovered later, after more pestering, that it wasn't the only medal for bravery Papa had won.

Maman revealed to me one morning as we were driving down to Folkestone for our New Year visit to the Aunties – Auntie Pish and Auntie Snowdrop, as we called them – that Auntie Snowdrop had Papa's other medals.

"She'll show you, I expect," she said, "if you ask. She's very proud of them."

I knew they had a photo of Papa in his RAF uniform. It was in a silver frame on the mantelpiece in their sitting room, always polished up and gleaming. He looked serious, frowning slightly as if some shadow was hanging over him. There were scarlet poppies lying scattered around the photograph. It was like a shrine, I thought. Auntie Pish was the loud one, talkative and bossy, forever telling me I should be tidier, and blaming Maman for it. She would chuck me under the chin and arrange my collar and tie – we always dressed up in our best for these visits – and she'd tell me, her voice catching, how alike we were, my Papa and I.

I'd often stand in front of that photo and try to see myself in my Papa's face. He had a moustache and high cheekbones, deep-set eyes, and in the photo his skin looked darker than mine too. Maman had told me that his hair was frizzy like mine. But most of his hair was hidden under his cap. In his RAF uniform with his cap perched on his head, he was simply a hero to me, a Spitfire pilot, like a god almost, not like me at all.

I dreaded these visits, and I could tell, even though she didn't ever say it, that Maman did too. For me though there was always Jasper to look forward to. He was their little white Jack Russell terrier with black eyes, bouncy and yappy and funny. I loved him, and he loved me. Every time we left I wanted to take him with us. On the journey home I'd go on and on about having a Jasper of our own, but Maman wouldn't hear of it. "Dogs!" she'd say. "They make a mess, they smell, they have fleas which is why they scratch. And they lick themselves all over in public. *Répugnant! Abhorrent! Dégoûtant!*" (She knew a lot of French words for disgusting!) "And they bite. Why would I want a dog? Why would anyone want a dog?"

I remember this visit better than any of the others, maybe because of the medals, or maybe because it was the last. As we drove towards Folkestone, Maman's nerves, as usual, were getting the better of her. I could tell because she was grinding the gears and cursing the car, in French, a sure sign with her. She was becoming more preoccupied with every mile. She was smoking one cigarette after another – she always smoked frantically when she was anxious. She started telling me what I must and must not say, how I must behave. She was never like this at home, only on our way to Folkestone to see the Aunties.

Once we arrived outside their bungalow she spent long minutes putting on her make-up and powdering her nose. When she finished she clicked her powder compact shut and turned to me with a sigh, a smile of resignation on her face. "Well, how do I look?" she asked, cheerier now. "Armour on, brave face on. 'Once more unto the breach, dear friends, once more' – that's from Shakespeare, *Henry the Fifth* – your Papa said that when we visited them together that first time, and every time afterwards too. It's what I have to remember, Michael. The Aunties may not be easy, but they adored your Papa. He was the centre of their lives, just as he was for me too. We are all the family they have now, now that he's gone. We mustn't forget that. I don't think they ever got over your Papa's death, you know. So they and I, we have that in common too. We miss him every day of our lives."

Maman had never spoken about Papa to me like this before, never once talked about her feelings until that moment. I think she might have said more, but then we saw

Auntie Snowdrop come scurrying down the path and out of the front gate, waving to us, Jasper running on ahead of her, yapping at the gulls in the garden, scattering them to the wind. "Oh God, that dog," Maman whispered under her breath. "And those horrible elves are still there in the front garden."

"Garden gnomes, Maman," I said. "They're garden gnomes, and I like them, specially the one that's fishing. And I like Jasper, too." I was opening the car door by now. "It's the rock cakes I don't like. The currants are as hard as nails."

"Won't you have another rock cake, Michael dear?" Maman said, imitating Auntie Pish's high-pitched tremulous voice and very proper English accent. "There's plenty left, you know. And mind your crumbs. *Pish*, you're getting them all over the carpet."

We got out of the car still laughing, as Jasper came scuttling along the pavement towards us, Auntie Snowdrop close behind him, her eyes full of welcoming tears. For her sake I made myself look as happy as I could to see her again too – and with Auntie Snowdrop, to be honest, that was not at all difficult. A bit 'doolally' she may have been, 'away with the fairies' – that was how Auntie Pish often described her – but she was always loving towards Maman and me, thoughtful and kind. To meet Auntie Pish though, I always had to steel myself, and I could see Maman did too. She was standing there now at the front door waiting for us as we came up the path. I bowed my head to avoid the bristly kiss.

"*Pish*, we thought you'd be here an hour ago," she said. "What kept you?" We were usually met with a reprimand of one kind or another. "Well, you're here now, I suppose," she went on. "Better late than never. You'd better come along in. Just in time for elevenses. The rock cakes are waiting." She tightened my tie and arranged my collar. "That's better, Michael dear. Still not the tidiest of boys, are we? I made the rock cakes specially, you know. Plenty to go round." Then she shouted to Auntie Snowdrop, "Martha, do make sure you shut that gate properly, won't you! *Pish*, she's always leaving it open. She's so forgetful these days. Come along!"

Maman didn't dare look at me and I didn't dare look at her.

Rock Cakes and Snowdrops

WHENEVER I CAME TO VISIT, JASPER ALWAYS TREATED
me like his best friend. He sat by my feet
under the kitchen table, and surreptitiously
ate all the rock cakes I gave him. He chewed
away secretly, though sometimes a little too

noisily, on the currants, licked his lips, then waited for more, his eyes wide with hope and expectation.

The chatter round the table echoed the last visit, and the one before, and the one before, as it always did. Auntie Pish did most of the talking, of course, and loudly because she was a bit deaf, peppering Maman and me with questions about my progress at school. She wanted only the good news – we knew that – so that's what we told her: winning a prize for effort, singing a solo in the carol service again, being top scorer in the football team.

She interrupted her interrogation from time to time with critical observations about my upbringing. "He's still not very big, is he?" she said to Maman. "*Pish.* I still don't think you feed him enough, you know. That's what we think, isn't it, Martha?"

It always came as something of a surprise to me when she called Auntie Snowdrop by her proper name. I had to think twice. Their names were too alike anyway, Martha and Mary. Perhaps that was why Maman and I had given them nicknames in the first place. "We shall need more milk from the larder, Martha," she went on, and then much louder, "I said, we want more milk, Martha." Auntie Pish's solution to her own deafness was to presume everyone else was deaf too.

Auntie Snowdrop was looking down at me adoringly, clearly not paying any attention to her elder sister. In all the years we'd visited, Auntie Snowdrop had said very little to me or to anyone – she let her sister do all the talking for both of them. But she'd always sit beside me, often with her arm around me, laying her hand gently on my hair from time to time. I think she just loved to touch it.

"Martha! The milk!"

Auntie Snowdrop got up and scuttled away apologetically. Auntie Pish reached out and chucked me under the chin, shaking her head sadly. "So like your father you are," she said. "Bigger ears though. His ears didn't stick out so much." But her mind was soon on other things. "And don't go helping yourself to my prune juice again," she called out after Auntie Snowdrop. Then confidentially to us, "She does you know. *Pish*, Martha's an awful thief when it comes to my prune juice. I have to keep my eye on these things. I have to keep my eye on everything."

Maman and I had worked out over the years how not to look at one another whenever prune juice or rock cakes were mentioned. The giggles would well up inside of us, threatening to break out. It helped that I was a little bit frightened of Auntie Pish – Maman was wary too, I think. Auntie Pish could be cruel, with Auntie Snowdrop in particular. Maman and I both disliked the way she treated Auntie Snowdrop, putting her down all the time. We hated especially how she'd talk about her behind her back.

In the sitting room after 'elevenses', as the Aunties always called the mid-morning break for tea and rock cakes, Auntie Pish would preside grandly in her armchair by the fire in her voluminous dress – she was a big woman anyway and always wore dresses that seemed to overflow in every direction. She'd hold court while Auntie Snowdrop made the lunch out in the kitchen. Auntie Snowdrop would be humming away as she worked, tunes I often recognised, because they were songs she'd taught me too: 'Down by the Sally Gardens', maybe – which was my favourite – or 'Danny Boy', or 'Speed Bonny Boat'. She was always humming or singing something. She had a very tuneful voice, sweet and soft and light, a voice that suited her.

Lunch was always the same on our visits: corned beef and bubble and squeak. And for pudding we had custard with brown sugar, because years before, when I was about three, Maman had told Auntie Snowdrop this was my favourite meal. Over lunch Auntie Snowdrop would fuss over me like a mother hen, making sure I had enough. The trouble was that I had very quickly had quite enough. At nine years old, I no longer liked corned beef and bubble and squeak, and I had gone off custard years ago. I hated the stuff, but I'd never had the nerve to tell her, and nor had Maman.

That lunchtime I had to work my way through three helpings of custard. Swallowing the last few spoonfuls was hard, so hard. I knew I mustn't leave anything in my bowl, that it must be scraped clean, that it would upset Auntie Snowdrop if it wasn't, and also invoke the wrath of Auntie Pish, whose favourite mantra at meal times was always, 'Waste not, want not'.

After lunch we went down to the beach as usual, and as usual Auntie Snowdrop took a bunch of snowdrops with her, snowdrops I'd helped pick with her from the garden – they grew in a great white carpet all around the garden gnomes. Jasper hated gulls, all gulls. He chased them fruitlessly up and down the beach, yapping at every one of them, returning to us exhausted but happy, and still yapping. We tramped together along the beach until Auntie Pish decided she had found just the right place. She waved her walking stick imperiously out to sea. "This'll do, Martha," she said. "Get on with it then."

Every year until now Auntie Snowdrop had performed the ceremony herself, but this time she turned to me. "I think maybe Michael should do it," she said, and she handed me the flowers. "He's old enough, don't you think? And after all, he was your father. Would you like to do it, Michael?"

Auntie Pish was clearly surprised, as we were, at how Auntie Snowdrop had suddenly taken the initiative, and she didn't like it one bit. She waved her stick at me impatiently. "Very well," she snapped. "If you're going to do it, then get on with it. But look out for the waves. Don't go getting your feet wet, Michael."

I took the flowers from Auntie Snowdrop and walked down to the water's edge.

I did it just as she had done it every year I could remember. I reached out and dropped the snowdrops into the sea one by one. Some the waves took away, others were washed at once back up onto the beach, and left stranded round my feet.

I felt Maman beside me, her arm around my shoulder. "Your Papa adored snowdrops, you know," she whispered.

"Is he really out there, Maman?" I asked her then. "Is that where his Spitfire went down?"

"Somewhere in the Channel, *chéri*," she replied. "No one quite knows where. But it doesn't matter, does it? He's with us always."

We turned back then and walked up the beach towards the Aunties.

Auntie Snowdrop had her handkerchief to her mouth. I could see she was crying quietly.

"Time for tea," Auntie Pish said. "Martha, would you please stop that dog yapping?

He's driving me mad. Come along. And do keep up, Martha, don't drag along behind so much. *Pish!*" And she strode off up the beach, stabbing her stick into the pebbles as she went. "Come along, come along."

Auntie Snowdrop caught my eye, smiled and raised her eyebrows, enduring the moment. She was telling me in her own silent way, don't worry. I'm used to it. I smiled back in solidarity.

The walk home took a while, a bit longer than usual. That was when I noticed Auntie Snowdrop was wheezing a bit, that she had to stop from time to time to catch her breath, so much so that in the end I left Jasper to run on ahead, and went back to keep her company. She smiled her thanks at me and took my hand in hers. She held on to me to steady herself, I remember that. And her hand was so cold.

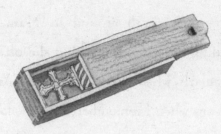

Just like his Papa was

AS I SAT THERE AT TEA-TIME IN THE SITTING ROOM
I couldn't wait to be gone. They clinked
their teaspoons on their cups and talked, and
talked, and went on talking, on and on, about
what I neither knew nor cared. Auntie Pish

was doing most of the talking and Maman looked about as fed up as I felt. I kept looking up at the photo of Papa on the mantelpiece, at the poppies all around it. Maman was twiddling her ring, something she often did, particularly when she was with the Aunties. That was when I remembered the medal I had found in the box when we'd moved house a few weeks before.

Maman must have guessed my thoughts, or read them perhaps. Suddenly she put her hand on mine, and interrupted Auntie Pish, who was not used to being interrupted.

"Sorry, Auntie Mary, but I've just remembered…" she began. Auntie Pish did not look at all pleased. "Auntie Martha. Roy's medals – the ones I let you have, remember?

He's got one of his own at home, haven't you, *chéri*? But I know he'd love to see the others sometime. Do you mind?"

"Of course I don't. They're upstairs," Auntie Snowdrop replied. "I'll fetch them at once, shall I?"

"Yes, Martha," Auntie Pish said, "you go and fetch them. And while you're about it, bring us the last of the rock cakes from the kitchen, will you? I see we have empty plates. Don't be long."

Auntie Snowdrop folded her napkin neatly, got up and went out. Auntie Pish shook her head. "She's always polishing those medals," she grumbled. "I don't know why she bothers – it only makes her sad. She still gets so upset and depressed: won't get up in the morning, won't eat her food, hardly speaks to me for days on end. If it wasn't for choir practice I sometimes think she'd give up the ghost altogether. I mean, Roy died over nine years ago now. The war was a long time ago. We have to put it all behind us, that's what I keep trying to tell her. It's water under the bridge, I tell her. Well I mean, there's no need for any more sadness, is there? No point. What's done is done. You can't bring him back, can you?"

Maman looked long at Auntie Pish before she spoke. Then she said very quietly: "Happiness, I think, is like Humpty Dumpty in that poem I used to read to Michael. 'All the King's horses, and all the King's men, couldn't put Humpty together again...' Once it is broken, you can't just put happiness together again. It is not possible."

Auntie Pish didn't know what to say, and for a change she said nothing. She cleared her throat and drank some more tea. Auntie Pish silenced. It was a rare and wonderful moment. It cheered me up no end. I almost felt like clapping, but then we heard Auntie Snowdrop coming slowly back downstairs. She came into the sitting room, carrying a wooden pencil box, holding it out in front of her, with the greatest of care, in both hands. Her eyes never left it as she put it down on the coffee table.

"Well, open it then, Martha," Auntie Pish told her impatiently. "It won't bite." Auntie Snowdrop slid back the lid and took it off.

There were three medals lying there on cotton wool, the King's face looking up at me from each one.

"You see how shiny I keep them?" Auntie Snowdrop was touching them with her fingertips. "Your Papa, I always thought he looked a bit like the King – except for the moustache, of course. I never liked his moustache. He said it made him look older, more like a proper fighter pilot. I never wanted him to go to war, you know. I told him. But he wouldn't listen to his old Auntie. This was his pencil case when he was a boy. He had it all through his school days." Then she looked up at me and fixed me with a gaze of such intensity that I've never forgotten it. "You'll never go to war, will you, Michael?" she said.

"No, Auntie," I told her, because that's what I knew she wanted me to say.

"Good. You don't need to, you know," she said, "because you'll have all these medals when I've gone, so you won't ever need to go to war to get them, like your Papa did."

"Oh Martha," Auntie Pish said. "Don't go on so. You'll upset the boy."

"And you will keep them polished for me," Auntie Snowdrop said, quite ignoring her sister.

"Course I will," I said.

"He's a good kind boy," Auntie Snowdrop said, reaching out and touching my hair. "Just like his Papa was. He has the same face, same lovely hair, just the same." She glanced up at the photo, and then back at me again. She took my hand, gripping it tight as she spoke to me. "But always remember, Michael, it's not the face that matters, not the skin, not the hair, it's what lies beneath. You have to look deeper, Michael, behind. Look through the glass, through the photo, and you'll find out who your Papa really was. Remember what I said now, won't you?"

We were driving back to London an hour or so later when Maman told me. "Auntie Snowdrop's not very well. She's going to have to go into hospital in a week or so for an operation – I think Auntie Pish is very worried about her."

"She didn't sound like it to me," I said. "She was horrible to her, she's always horrible to her."

"I know," Maman replied. "But you have to remember, *chéri*, those two, they've been together, lived together, all their lives. They need one another. I doubt they could ever live without each other, not now. Auntie Pish is an hour or so older, that's all. No twins were ever less identical, that's for sure. Your Papa used to say to me that they were like two sides of the same coin. And he knew them better than anyone."

I looked down at the snowdrop I'd been given when we left and remembered how long and tight Auntie Snowdrop had hugged me when we said our goodbyes, how she'd stood there waving us off, how frail she had suddenly seemed.

"She will be all right, won't she?" I asked.

"Let's hope so," Maman said, but she said nothing more.

As I pressed the snowdrop into my diary later that night, I turned back through the pages and found the many others I had brought back from our visits to Folkestone over the years. I saw how they were lace-thin and transparent with age – like the skin on Auntie Snowdrop's hand, I thought. I hoped then that this wouldn't be the last snowdrop she would give me.

That night I lay in bed picturing Papa's face in my mind, doing what Auntie Snowdrop had told me, trying to discover the man behind the photo, to look deeper. I fell asleep still trying, still wondering.

Down by the Sally Gardens

I CAME OUT OF SCHOOL — IT MUST HAVE BEEN A few months later, I suppose — after one of those days when everything had gone right, and there weren't many days like that. We'd had extra playtime because two teachers were away with the flu. So there was lots of time for football and hopscotch and marbles in the playground. No sums, no spelling tests, no dictations, no standing in the corner. Best of all, there was Maman waiting for me at the school gates when I came out.

Although I was pleased to see her, it was odd, because there was no reason for her to be there, none that I could think of anyway. I mean, there was no smog, so she couldn't have been worried about me crossing the road on my own. And she wasn't coming into school to see the teacher because I was in trouble, not so far as I knew. Maybe she'd come by because she was on her way to the shops and we'd stop off at the Milk Bar in the High Street, and I'd have a chocolate milkshake? Now that would be good! It had happened before once or twice.

As it turned out, that was exactly where we were going, not to the shops, she said, but straight to the Milk Bar, which was fine with me. Milkshakes were always a rare and real treat.

Maman seemed strangely distant somehow as we walked along. I was prattling on about how good school was when the teachers have flu, how the boys' toilets were flooded so we'd had to use the teachers' toilets, and that was great because there was a wooden seat, and a lock on the door, the paper was soft... but I could tell Maman wasn't listening to a word I was saying. All the way down the street she hardly spoke, which wasn't like her at all. I remembered then that she hadn't been smiling when she first saw me running across the playground towards her. And Maman always smiled and hugged me after school, always.

The milkshake was cold and long and gave me a headache because I drank it through the straw too fast. I stopped drinking for a moment and glanced up at her. She was looking down at me and I knew from her eyes that she was about to tell me something she didn't want to tell me.

"It's about Auntie Martha, Michael," she began.

"What?" I said. Maman rarely called the Aunties – either of them – by their proper names. I knew already what was coming.

"It is difficult for me to tell you, *chéri*, but you have to know," she went on. "You know Auntie Martha had her operation a while ago, on her lungs. Well everything seemed to be all right. She was getting better..."

"She's died, hasn't she?" I said.

Maman nodded. "In her sleep last night, that's what Auntie Mary said on the phone this morning. Very peaceful. I'm so sorry, Michael. You liked her a lot, didn't you? And I know she loved you. She was very proud of you, you and your Papa. She was a sweet lady, always kind and thoughtful. There's a funeral the day after tomorrow, in Folkestone, but you don't have to come, if you'd rather not."

"I'll come," I told her. I didn't finish my milkshake.

I had never been to a funeral before, I didn't know what to expect. I certainly hadn't expected a huge church packed with people, hundreds of them, the ladies in hats, and the men, stiff in dark suits and black ties, their hair slicked down. Some had to stand all the way through the service because there was no room for them to sit down. I could hardly believe it, all these people there for my Auntie Snowdrop. I sat in the front pew between Maman and Auntie Pish, with Jasper beside her. The coffin rested on trestles only a few feet away – all of us together for the last time.

I kept thinking how wrong I had been to assume that my two funny old Aunties knew almost no one in the world except us. Certainly we had never met anyone else at their house when we came on our visits, no friends, no other relatives. They didn't talk of anyone else either. There weren't any other relatives that I was aware of anyway. Now, here were all these people, and all of them Auntie Snowdrop's friends, a whole church full of them. I had imagined she lived a solitary and cheerless sort of existence with Auntie Pish, behind the white picket fence of their little house by the sea, with only Jasper for company, and the gulls that wheeled over the chimney or sat on the heads of the gnomes in the garden and cried to the wind.

All through the hymns and songs and prayers – we sang 'Down by the Sally Gardens' for her – I couldn't take my eyes off the coffin. It was so close to me that I could almost reach out and touch it. I was sure that she was lying there inside and listening to everything. And I was sure she knew I was there. I had to say something. I could only think of one thing to say and I spoke it from my heart, silently, my eyes closed.

I thanked her for all the snowdrops she'd given me, and promised her I'd keep them in my diary, pressed there forever so I wouldn't forget her. As I sat there, I kept seeing her, clear as clear in my mind, her hand still waving to us as we drove away after that last visit.

When the church service was over, everyone gathered around the grave. Jasper was there too, lying at my feet, head on his paws. I stood there between Maman and Auntie Pish. Auntie Pish had her arm round my shoulder and I could feel she was trembling. I looked up into her face and saw that she was crying. I had never imagined that Auntie Pish could cry. In all the faces I saw around the graveside that afternoon, there was such warmth and love for Auntie Snowdrop. I felt sadder at that moment than ever before in my whole life, and maybe ever since.

Grief is Grey

THERE WAS A GREAT GATHERING IN THE CHURCH
hall afterwards where everyone talked loudly
into each other's faces, sipping their tea and
chewing away all the while on Auntie Pish's
rock buns — she must have made hundreds of

them. I kept close to Maman for protection, hid behind her whenever I could. Everyone was kind, but too full of questions I didn't want to answer. They all wanted to talk about their memories of Auntie Snowdrop, of the songs they'd sung with her, the concerts they'd been to, the coastal walks they'd done. But I had my own memories, and I'd keep them to myself. Again and again they kept telling me how proud she was of me, how she never stopped talking about me.

The tea party seemed to go on forever, and would have been quite unbearable if I hadn't thought up the brilliant excuse that Jasper needed a walk. Maman said it was a good idea, but not to be too long. So I escaped and we went running off together along the beach. I ran till I could run no more. I skimmed stones, Jasper barked at the gulls, and afterwards we both sat side by side and stared out to sea. It was a dull day, the grey of the sky meeting the grey of the sea on the horizon. It seemed as if Auntie Snowdrop's death had left the world a colourless place. Grief is grey, I discovered that day.

Eventually Maman came out to find me and fetch me back into the hall. I couldn't face those people again, I told her. I just wanted to go home. To my great relief, she agreed that we had stayed long enough. She told Auntie Pish I had to be at school the next day and that I had some homework to do,

so we'd better be getting home. Auntie Pish came out and walked us to the car, carrying Jasper under her arm.

"Who were all those people in there?" I asked her.

"All your Auntie Martha's friends," she said. "Martha sang in the church choir, you know, and in the bath too every night. She had a lovely voice. She loved singing – and football, did you know that? Her two great passions: singing and football. Her favourite team was Arsenal – The Arsenal. She always said I had to call them The Arsenal."

"Football?" I said, amazed. "She never told me that."

"Didn't she? Oh, she was a real Gunners

fan, but she kept it to herself. Let me tell you, young man, there's a great deal you don't know about your Auntie Martha, a very great deal. Oh, she was a dark horse that one, but..." Her voice faltered then and she turned away. "She was the best of sisters, and the best friend I've ever had." She was still tearful when she hugged me goodbye, Jasper licking my ear as she did so.

"You'll be all right?" Maman asked her.

"*Pish*, I've got Jasper, haven't I?" she replied, recovering herself as best she could, and trying to smile through her tears. "Jasper and I, we shall be fine. But you will come and see us, won't you? And thanks for being here today. She'll be so happy you were with us." She bent down then and chucked me under the chin. "Your Auntie Snowdrop loved you, you know, like a mother loves a son, that much." She hugged Maman then. "And they say that no one loves anyone more than that."

"Quite true," Maman said.

"But," I said, "how did you know we called her Auntie Snowdrop? We thought it was our secret."

"I have ears," Auntie Pish said, reaching out and tugging gently at my ear lobe. "This boy of yours, he talks to Jasper sometimes, often far too loudly. I may be deaf, but I'm not daft. Boys are always too loud. Don't worry, I like being Auntie Pish. It suits me, and she loved being Auntie Snowdrop." She laughed then. "Truth will out in the end. Secrets, like the seasons, they never last, you know. And by the way, Poodle, I shall be sending you a parcel in the post, a present from Auntie Snowdrop; or maybe I'll bring it up myself one day, turn up out of the blue at your house. I'd like that. I haven't been to London in ten years or more – not since the War, come to think of it." She put Jasper down. "Come along, dear," she said to him. "Let's go home."

And off she went up the hill, her stick tapping, Jasper running along ahead. He did stop once to look back at us – his way of saying goodbye, or maybe of telling me that he was thinking what I hoped he was thinking: that he really wanted to come home with me, but he couldn't.

Later, in the car on our way home, I was lost in my thoughts. Something was bothering me and I couldn't work out what it was, not for a while. Then it came to me. I asked Maman, "And how did she know I was called 'Poodle' at school? Did you tell her?"

"No, of course not," she said. "You must have told that dog, just like you told him about their names, too loudly, probably. She's really not as deaf as I thought. That'll teach you to talk to dogs, to tell them your secrets. You can't trust them, you know. How embarrassing, to be found out like that."

"But funny," I said.

"*Oui*, funny, *mon petit chou*," she laughed, "very funny."

All the way home, I was wondering what Auntie Pish was going to send me.

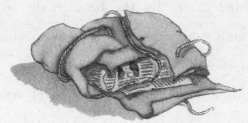

Auntie Snowdrop's Parcel

FIVE YEARS LATER – I'D HAVE BEEN ABOUT THIRTEEN by this time – and Auntie Snowdrop's parcel still hadn't arrived, and neither had Auntie Pish ever come to visit us in London. Maman always said she wouldn't, that she'd never leave Folkestone. To begin with, for the first few months after the funeral, I had hoped for the promised parcel with every post, but nothing came. By the time it did arrive, I'd long since forgotten about it. And even then, it didn't come in the post.

After Auntie Snowdrop's funeral, Auntie Pish seemed to lose heart. We went down to Folkestone to see her much more often, not to spread snowdrops on the sea – it didn't seem right to do that any more, not without Auntie Snowdrop there – but because Maman was worried about her. Auntie Pish's memory was not as good as it had been, that was becoming quite obvious to us. She seemed more confused every time we visited. She kept talking on about Auntie Snowdrop as if she was still alive, and sometimes – which was quite unlike her old self – she'd burst into tears and become very anxious and agitated. She'd say such strange things through her tears, snatches of half-lost memories that neither of us knew anything about, mostly about her father, and her mother too.

After one of our visits I wrote something she'd said to us down in my diary when I got home, because it upset me to see her so like this. "Father wouldn't listen, you know. I told him I'd have to go with her, that someone had to look after her. But oh no, he wouldn't listen, he wouldn't listen. It broke Mother's heart, broke my heart too." We had no idea what she was talking about.

As these episodes became more frequent,

and made our visits more troubling, I wanted
less and less to go down there to see her. I
made lots of excuses not to go, football usually.
I'm not proud of that now. Maman was not
as faint-hearted as I was. She continued to go
down to see her on her own most Saturdays,
insisting that Auntie Snowdrop and Papa
would never have wanted her left alone, that
both Aunties in their own ways had been very
kind to her when she needed it most. Then
Auntie Pish broke her leg. We had a phone
call from the hospital and both of us went
down there as soon as we could.

Maman and I sat either side of her bed
as she complained bitterly about the food,
how the nurses kept waking her up to give
her pills when she wanted to sleep, and how

she didn't want the pills anyway. *"Pish,"* she said. "I don't need pills. I want to get out of here. I want to go home." But mostly it was Jasper she complained about. "It was Jasper who broke my leg. It was all his fault, his and the postman's. I heard the postman come whistling down the path, so I went to the door just like I usually do to pick the letters up from the mat before Jasper gets to them. And what happens? Jasper comes charging down the hallway, barges past me and trips me up. If Martha had been there, it wouldn't have happened. She always goes to the door." She started crying then. "She's not at home, you know. Where's Martha gone? Where's Martha gone? Who's going to look after Jasper? And there's the geraniums, the frost will get them if I don't fetch them in soon."

"Don't worry, Mary," said Maman. "Michael and I will look after everything, won't we, *chéri*?"

"You will? You'll look after Jasper and the geraniums? You'd like to look after Jasper, wouldn't you, Michael?"

Would I! Would I! I could hardly contain my joy.

I turned to Maman. She didn't look happy.

"It'll only be for a week or so, I promise," Auntie Pish told us. "I'll be right as rain in a week or so, fit as a fiddle, you'll see."

So we went up to Auntie Pish's house afterwards, and brought her geraniums in. I took Jasper for a run on the beach while Maman tidied the house and turned off the water and locked up. That evening we drove back to London with Jasper in the back of the car. I was over the moon. Jasper was coming home with me! At last I had a dog of my own. Jasper kept smiling up at me, panting with happiness.

But Maman made it quite clear she did not feel the same. "That dog stays downstairs, Michael. Do you hear?" she said. "I will not have him up in your bedroom, and he is not allowed on the chairs in the sitting room, and if he makes messes, you clear them up. *Tu comprends*?" She sighed deeply. "I just hope that leg of hers gets better soon like she said."

But it didn't. It took forever to heal. Maman was back and forth to Folkestone for weeks. Then, while Auntie Pish was still in hospital, she got pneumonia. After that she was too weak to look after herself. Maman found her a place in a nursing home just outside the town – not an easy task because Auntie Pish was very particular. She insisted she had to be able to see the sea from her bedroom window like she could back in her own home.

Meanwhile, at home in Philbeach Gardens, Jasper had become one of the family. He slept on my bed every night, despite all Maman's protests, bit the post as it came in through the door, and chased the cats in the park – there weren't any gulls. Maman never came to like him. She did get used to him, feed him even, take him out for his walks sometimes. But whenever I wasn't at school, Jasper became my constant companion. He came to football with me, chased the ball and made a nuisance of himself. We got on so well, knew each other's thoughts almost. I had the strangest feeling sometimes that he and I were meant for each other, almost related, that somehow Auntie Snowdrop had arranged the whole thing.

Sometimes, on Saturdays, I did go down to the nursing home with Maman, when football was rained off, or when I just couldn't come up with a good enough excuse to get out of it. I never looked forward to going because we just had to sit there in her tiny box of a room – a bed, a bedside table and one chair. I had to sit at the end of her bed and listen to her rambling on for hours. She treated Maman now rather as she had treated Auntie Snowdrop. Maman was kind and attentive and endlessly patient, but as with Auntie Snowdrop, there were never any thanks. Auntie Pish just took her more and more for granted. She was even sharp with Maman sometimes. She could be really nasty.

When I complained about this to Maman, and said she shouldn't put up with it, she'd always make excuses for her. She'd say that Auntie Pish was very old and that old people get like that; that it was only natural that she might be a bit difficult and truculent at her age, how she'd lived through a lot, and had a heart of gold underneath. Maman was always so forgiving.

It was on one of these visits, that out of the blue I received at last Auntie Snowdrop's long-forgotten parcel. Wrapped in brown paper and tied up neatly with string, it was lying there on Auntie Pish's bed when

Maman and I walked into her room. "Auntie Martha wants you to have this," she said. All these years later – nearly five years now – she still talked of her sister as if she was alive. "She's wrapped it up specially for you. It's breakable, so take care how you open it."

I didn't bother about being careful. I pulled and tugged and jerked at the string until it came away. Underneath the brown paper, the parcel was neatly wrapped in layer after layer of newspaper, each layer folded over carefully. It took forever to open it. I couldn't do it fast enough. It felt like a book of some kind.

Read it, his eyes were telling me

IT WASN'T UNTIL I FELT THE GLASS THAT I KNEW it for what it was. There, looking up at me, was Papa's face. The frame was not polished, I noticed, as it always had been before on the mantelpiece in their sitting room in

Folkestone. I felt Maman's hand on my shoulder.

"He looks pleased to see you, *chéri*," she said.

When Auntie Pish fell asleep soon after, we crept out of her room and drove home. I sat in the car with the parcel on my lap all the way back to London, opening up the wrapping from time to time to look at Papa.

"I'll polish that frame when we get home," Maman said.

"I'll do it," I told her.

In the end Maman and I did it together, on the kitchen table, with Jasper up on a chair beside us, watching. Maman did the hard work, putting the polish on, and rubbing the tarnish off. It took some doing. Then I had the satisfaction of shining it up, breathing and polishing till it gleamed. Once it was done I took it up to my bedroom and stood it up on my desk. I sat there and stared at Papa. That was when Auntie Snowdrop's words came back to me – I hadn't thought about them in a long while. "Always remember, Michael, it's not the face that matters, not the skin, not the hair, it's what lies beneath. You have to look deeper, Michael, behind. Look through the glass, through the photo, and you'll find out who your Papa really was."

I looked hard into Papa's face, into his eyes, trying all I could to know the man behind the glass, behind the photo, behind the eyes.

Jasper was with me, snuffling around my feet. I wasn't paying him any attention, which was why, I suppose, he decided to jump up onto my desk and shove his nose into my face, knocking the photograph over as he did so. I heard the glass shatter as it fell.

· "Get off, Jasper," I shouted, pushing him aside angrily. I'd never been so angry with him before. As I was standing the frame up again the glass fell out onto my desk in several pieces. I've often thought since that Jasper might have done it on purpose, because he knew, because he was trying to tell me, because Auntie Snowdrop had told him all about it, and he knew that's what Auntie Snowdrop wanted him to do. He wanted me to find it, and so did Auntie Snowdrop. That's why he broke it. That's what I think, anyway.

It was the first time I'd seen Papa's face

not through glass. He was already somehow more real to me, closer and more alive without the glass in between us. The photo was loose in the frame now, and had slipped down. I noticed there was one small piece of broken glass still trapped there in the bottom corner of the frame. I tried to prise it out with the point of my pencil, but I couldn't do it. I'd have to open up the frame at the back if I was going to get it out.

I hadn't really noticed, not until now, but the back of the frame was nothing but a piece of cardboard, held in place by a few rusty-looking pins. All I had to do was to pull these out one by one and the cardboard came away easily enough. I had expected to see simply the back of the photograph, but there was something else there, a writing pad about the same size as the photo. On the front it said, 'Basildon Bond', in fancy printing, and below it, written in pencil, in large capital letters:

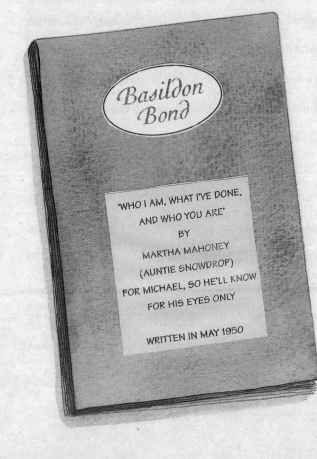

Basildon Bond

'WHO I AM, WHAT I'VE DONE, AND WHO YOU ARE' BY MARTHA MAHONEY (AUNTIE SNOWDROP) FOR MICHAEL, SO HE'LL KNOW FOR HIS EYES ONLY

WRITTEN IN MAY 1950

It took me a little while to cast my mind back, to work it out. This must have been written then about a month or so before she died, because I knew that was in June of 1950. (I checked later in my diary and I was right about that.)

She'd hidden it behind the photo for me to find. Behind the photo! Behind the photo!

Maman called up from downstairs. "*Chéri*, I've got to go down to the shops. Have you got that dog up there? I'd better take him with me. He hasn't had his walk yet. You'll be all right on your own?"

"I'll be fine," I told her. I opened the door to let Jasper out. He didn't seem to want to go even when Maman whistled for him. She had to shout for him more than once. Even then he went only because I pushed him out – I was still cross with him. He gave me a long last look before he left. *Read it*, his eyes were telling me. *Read it*. Then he was gone, scuttling down the stairs. I heard the front door close after them.

I was alone. I went back to my desk, picked up Auntie Snowdrop's writing pad, sat on my bed, pillows piled behind me, rested the pad on my knees, and opened it. My heart was pounding. I knew even as I began to read – and I have no idea how I knew – that my life would be changed forever, that after I'd read this I would never be the same person again.

Who I am, What I've done, and Who you are

I'm telling you this, writing it down for you, Michael, because we all have a right to know who we are. I should have told you myself, face to face a long time ago. Early on, when you were little, I always thought you were too young – or that was my excuse. And then as you grew up,

I didn't know how to tell you. I never had the courage, that's the truth of it. I should have told your Maman too, but I could never quite bring myself to do that either.

Now that I've been told in the hospital that time is running out for me, that I have only a few months left, I thought this was the one last thing I had to do. Somehow I had to tell you, and there seemed to me only one way to do it. I would put it all down on paper, and arrange things, if I could, so that one day you would find it and read it for yourself. I did try to point you in the right direction. I did tell you where to look, didn't I? Look behind the face. Remember?

I could have given it to your Auntie Mary for her to give to you, but I don't want her to know I'm doing this – I don't like to upset her. And anyway, as you'll soon discover, this is between you and me. Your Auntie Mary knows the truth of everything that's written here – she was so much part of the whole story – but she's always told me it was best to keep it as a secret between her and me, just the two of us, and so it always has been. That way, she thinks, no one comes to any harm.

Until just recently, until my last visit to the hospital, when they told me, I suppose I always used to believe she was right. But not any more. I think there are some things that are so much part of who we are, that we should know about them, that we have a right to know about them.

If you're reading this at all, Michael, then it means you've found my little writing pad behind the photo of your Papa, just as I intended you to. Please don't be too upset. Read it again from time to time as you get older. I think it will be easier to understand as you get older. It's not so much that wisdom comes with age – as we older people rather like to believe. It doesn't. But I am sure that as we grow up we do become more able to understand ourselves and other people a little better. We are more able to deal with difficulty, and to forgive perhaps. If you are anything like me, Michael – and I think you probably are – I am sure you will become more understanding and forgiving as the years pass. I hope so, because I'm sure that it's only in forgiving that we find real peace of mind.

I'm writing this as well, because I want you to feel proud of who you are, and proud of the people who made you. Believe you me, you have much to feel proud about. Perhaps my problem has always been that I have never been proud enough of who I am. I am a bit muddle-headed, simple-minded perhaps, and foolish – certainly foolish. I have always allowed my sister, whom I love dearly, to do most of my thinking for me. It's just how we are and always have been. She's been the strong one all my life, my rock you might say. I know she can seem a bit of a know-all, a bit overbearing; but as you'll soon discover, she has looked after me, stood by me when no one else would. There's a lot more to Mary than meets the eye – that's true of everyone, I think. I should have been quite lost in this life without her. So here's our story, hers and mine – and most importantly, yours.

None of this will make sense if you don't

know to begin with how Mary and I were brought up, what kind of home we came from. We were born – Mary as you know, an hour or so before me – way up north in Scotland, in Aberdeenshire, in a grey old house in the countryside miles away from any town. I went into Aberdeen – which was less than twenty miles from our home – just once in my entire childhood, and then it was to the hospital to have my tonsils out. The countryside around us, and our village, was our whole world. We didn't speak English in our house, but a strange language they call 'Doric'. Not many people in our village spoke it. A few did, but only very few. I don't think anyone speaks it any more these days, which is a shame. Father insisted we spoke it, read it, and even said our prayers in it.

Father was a Minister of the Church – the Kirk we called it. He was rather disapproving and distant with us, a stern man. I don't think I can remember him smiling once. I can't even imagine it happening. Mother was kind enough with us, but she was very meek and mild. She lived, as we did, under Father's rules, under his shadow. It became clear to us as we grew up that she had to do what Father said in all things. She was truly fearful of him, I think, as Mary and I were too. He never beat us or harmed us, but he was always a brooding presence. He moved about the house like a ghost. Every time he came into the room it seemed that a cold draught came in with him.

So our childhood was spent mostly outside the

house, as far away from Father as possible. Outside – always providing we had done our homework and Father had checked it – we could wander free, just so long as we were back for meal times, our hands and faces clean. The countryside was a paradise for us, and we weren't alone in it. There were wounded creatures to care for: an owl with a broken wing, a chick fallen out of the nest, a lost duckling, a lizard that had lost its tail. At one time Mary and I had a secret animal hospital in a shed at the bottom of our garden, and lots of little patients. We had woods and fields to play in, hills to climb, streams to paddle in. Here we could lark about without fear of disapproval.

Mary and I became more and more inseparable

and protective of one another as we got older. At school we sat side by side and never played with anyone else in the playground unless we had to. I was always better at reading and singing, and Mary could do sums in her head without even thinking about it. We helped one another. So, when it came to homework, we expected to get the same mark, and of course we usually did.

Following my Dream

Both of us harboured very different dreams. I wanted to travel the world – I think I got my wanderlust, in part at least, from the stories of Robert Louis Stevenson, *Treasure Island* and *Travels with a Donkey*. I wanted to ride off to Edinburgh on a donkey, sail across the ocean to faraway places where I could be a singer or a dancer, or even join a circus – I loved acrobatics. Mary, on the other hand, wanted to grow up to be a teacher, to live her whole life in our village, walk the same fields and hills we could see from our bedroom window. She tried to dissuade me from following my dreams and always insisted I should stay here at home, so that she and I could be together and she could look after me. But I was determined to get away, somehow, anyhow.

So when the war began, in 1914, I took my chance. I was nearly eighteen by then. Many of the boys in the village were joining up and going overseas to France. So I decided to do the same, but as a nurse. I didn't tell anyone, not even Mary. I just went into town on the bus, volunteered, and signed up. They needed all the nurses they could get, I discovered. I had to report to Aberdeen in a week. Mary was furious with me when I got back, as I knew she would be – she has never liked me doing things on my own, certainly not without asking her first. Mother cried and begged me not to go. Surprisingly though, Father approved of what I'd done, and supported me. He said that, as a family, we couldn't stand idly by with the rest of the country going to war.

Mary and I had our first real argument. I always tried to avoid arguing with Mary, mostly because I always lost, but also because I knew it would only upset her. She said I was only joining up because I liked boys.

I denied it of course, but the trouble was that she was right, in a way. We'd both been very shy around boys, but at eighteen I found they wanted to talk to me and joke with me. They liked me, and the truth was that I liked being liked, and I liked them. I was discovering I was pretty. It's difficult for you to believe, I know, Michael, but I was really quite pretty in those days – in a quiet sort of a way. But I also wanted to become a nurse for other reasons, good reasons too.

I'd always loved looking after sick and wounded animals in the countryside, mostly wild animals. And sometimes I'd cared for the sickly lambs and calves on the farm down the lane from us. I could do the same I thought with the soldiers at the front, tend their wounds, be a comfort to them. And I could travel at the same time. I was determined that it was the right thing to do, and that I would do it whatever Mary said. She wouldn't speak to me for days before I went off to Aberdeen to join up and do my training as a nurse. She came all the way to the station with me, silent and sullen the whole while, but as the train came in she hugged me so tight that I knew I'd been forgiven. I waved her goodbye and off I went to war, feeling sad, not wanting to go, yet longing to see this new world out there, a world that I'd only ever read about in books or seen in pictures. And with me on the train were the young soldiers in their kilts, all as excited as I was. It seems so silly now, so senseless, when I think of

how many of them never came home again. But we had youth and hope in our hearts, and a song to sing. How we all sang on that train.

Within a few months I was out in Belgium, not France as it turned out, posted to a hospital a few miles behind the lines. Here we heard for the first time the rumble and pounding of the guns, theirs and ours, a dreadful overture of the horrors that were to come. We were near Ypres, outside a town called Poperinge. Almost at once we found ourselves looking after soldiers with dreadful wounds, dying soldiers. You cannot imagine the sights I saw, Michael, nor do I want you even to try to imagine them. Many nights I cried myself to sleep, and wondered how I could face the suffering I would have to witness again the next morning. I wrote every day to Mary and she always wrote back to me, her letters full of encouragement and love.

As I sat by the bedside, holding a dying soldier by the hand, trying to give what comfort I could, I could honestly feel Mary there beside me, helping me through it all. Some of the boys would ask me to write a letter home to a sweetheart or a mother. Often it was a last letter. I think they just wanted to feel that someone loved them.

Meet Jasper

*I*t was while I was with those poor wounded soldiers that I first understood, Michael, that when all's said and done, it's what we all want and need most: to love and to be loved.

Perhaps you're wondering by now why I'm telling you all this, rambling on as I am, what all this has to do with you? Well, I'm coming to that.

We nurses didn't get much time off duty, but when we did, we'd walk into Poperinge, and stroll around the town. It was somewhere to go. There wasn't much else to do, and it was just a blessed relief for us to be away from the hospital, for a few hours at least. That was when I first saw him. He was sitting outside a café in the sunshine with some of his pals, smoking a cigarette, having a drink. One of them called us over to join them. So we did. There were five or six soldier boys sitting there, and all of them keen to get to know us. You've got to remember there were hundreds of them out there, thousands, and hardly any girls from home. So we nurses were always rather popular wherever we went.

I noticed him first of course. There weren't many black soldiers in the army, very few in fact. But it wasn't just because he was black. He was the silent one, the only shy one there – the others were cheeky and cheerful, full of themselves, all banter and bravado. Not him. I liked him at once, liked his quietness. I felt easy with him. That's why, when we accepted their invitation to sit down with them at the café table, I turned and talked to him. He also happened to be the handsomest man I'd ever set eyes on. As it turned out he didn't have much to say for himself. I thought he wasn't interested in me. But when, an hour or so later, we got up to go, he stood up and held out his hand. When I took it, it was suddenly as if there was no one there but us, no one in the whole world but us.

He said: "I hope we'll meet again, Miss."

"I hope so too," I replied.

"I'll come back here when I can – if you will," he said.

"I will," I told him.

That first meeting had the strangest effect on me. After it, I seemed able to bear my nursing work in the hospital so much better. I felt somehow as if I was floating above it, above all the pain and suffering of those young men, that I had a new-found strength to deal with it, that I was passing this strength on to them. Just the thought of my soldier boy in the café kept me going. I still didn't even know his name.

I lived for my few hours of leave. Every week, I'd walk the couple of miles into Poperinge, to the café where we had met, and where I was quite sure we would meet again. Even as the months passed and he didn't come, I never doubted for a moment that he'd be there one day. I'd sit outside the café at the same table, drink tea and write another letter to Mary, and wait and watch the people go by. When he didn't come, and he didn't come, I was disappointed, of course I was, but I never despaired. One day soon he would turn up and I would be waiting. On that, I fixed all my hope.

It soon got round the hospital. I'd been seen sitting at the café again, and again, and again. My nursing friends knew what I was up to without having to ask, but they did ask of course. And I told them. I had nothing to hide – I didn't want to hide it. Every one of them had something to say about it. They'd come along sometimes and sit with me, and wait, and of course they teased me. Some of them said I shouldn't be 'mixing with that sort'. I ignored them. Others, the kinder ones, and that was most of them, tried to warn me, kept telling me I mustn't get my hopes up too much, that as like as not he'd have forgotten all about me by now, that's if he hadn't already been posted further away down the line. But one or two of my best friends did voice the only real fear I had, that the worst had happened, that he'd been killed.

Mary wrote to me saying, 'You should be sensible, Martha, and put your thinking cap on, and not lose your head over the first man you ever met. For goodness' sake, girl, you don't even know his name! And, I must say this, Martha – and I don't like saying it – from what you've told me about him in your letters, he is different from us, isn't he?'

I still have that letter. I kept all Mary's letters. Despite everything everyone said, everything Mary wrote, I held him in my head and my heart for all those months, and kept going back and back to the café whenever I could get a leave pass to go into town, which wasn't often. There were always too many casualties to look after, so that we were sometimes on duty seven days a week, week in week out. And always the guns growled and thundered in the distance, and at night the flares went up on the horizon, reminding me that my soldier boy was out there somewhere – alive or dead, I didn't know. I willed him safe. He would come back to me. He had to.

So you can imagine that I was over the moon with joy and relief, when I walked into the village square one sunny Sunday morning during a lull in the fighting, and found him sitting there at our table at the café, tucking into a huge plate of egg and chips. At his feet, I noticed, there was a small white dog with black eyes, gazing up longingly at each chip as it disappeared into his mouth. I stood there watching them both for a while before my soldier boy looked up and saw me. He stood up in a hurry, wiping his mouth with the back of his hand.

"I've been hoping you'd come," he said.

"What kept you?" I said.

"The war, I suppose. But it's quieter now. They gave us a few days' leave. Some of the lads went home, most of them. I came back instead to see you. I've been sitting here, waiting for you to come. This is my third plate of egg and chips. Still, I'm not complaining. When I'm in the trenches I dream of egg and chips, and a hot bath… and a beer," he added, laughing. He laughed easily.

Everything about him was so easy, so natural. The dog was jumping up, pawing at his leg. "All right, boy, all right. I think he wants to be introduced."

"I'm Martha," I told him.

"Meet Jasper," he said. "He's a German dog, really. Came over from the other side of No Man's Land a couple of weeks ago, just strolled across and jumped down into our trenches. They were shouting out after him, '*Komm* *zurück* Jasper!' Come back, Jasper, that is!

'*Komm' zurück!*' But we whistled him over and he just kept on coming. He's our Company dog now. Something like a Jack Russell terrier, isn't he? We adopted him and he's adopted us. I look after him. He likes to go where I go. Seems he likes our Tommy chips better than he liked their Fritz sausages, don't you, Jasper?"

Leroy Hamilton

*O*f course I can't pretend that was word for
word what he said – so I'm making it up a little
bit as I go along. But that was the gist of it. And
I can't remember how long we sat at that table
downing egg and chips, and beer. I had my first
ever sip of beer that day – Father would never

allow alcohol in the house back home. All I know is that we talked and talked.

After a while he took my hands in his. He had big, beautiful hands, hands that swallowed mine, that made me feel safe. He said he wanted to know all about me, everything. So I told him. He looked at me as I spoke, his eyes never leaving mine, as if they were windows into my life. I could tell that everything I said seemed to fascinate him, and that amazed me – I never imagined anyone could be that interested in my little world of home: in Aberdeenshire, in the strange Doric language we spoke at home, how Mary and I were like two sides of the same coin, how each would often know what the other was thinking before she even said it.

But when I began to tell him something

of my work in the hospital, I could see it hurt him to hear about it. So I didn't go on. Instead I told him that it was his turn, that I wanted to know all about him. But he wouldn't talk about himself, not then, no matter how hard I pressed him.

It was only bit by bit, over the next weeks and months, and over time since, that I've managed to piece together his life. And it's really his life I wanted to tell you about, Michael, because you already know all you need to know about mine. You'll understand why it's important soon enough. I'll tell you all I can, all I know.

His name was Leroy Hamilton. I'd draw you a picture of him if I could. I haven't even got a photograph of him. So words will have to do. He was twenty-two, older than me by four years. But he seemed a lot older. He was born in London – I don't know where and neither did he. All he could tell me about his family was that his father came from Barbados and was a sailor. His mother lived in Chatham, in Kent, near the docks. They had five children, and Leroy was the youngest. His father came and went, as sailors do, and so his mother had to bring the family up on her own. Then his father just stopped coming back. As a little boy, Leroy always imagined that he'd been drowned at sea, shipwrecked, otherwise why wouldn't he have come home? Anyway, after that, his mother began to drown her sorrows in drink. Leroy said he thought she died of sorrow, as much as from the drink.

So, at the age of five, Leroy found himself
an orphan, separated suddenly from all his
brothers and sisters – he never saw any of them
again – and taken off to a children's home,
to an orphanage in London. And that's where
Leroy grew up. It wasn't so bad. He used to
tell me that instead of just four brothers and
sisters, he had hundreds of them now. Like
all of them there, he had no mother and no
father, and he felt the ache of that inside

him, but in the orphanage they were all in it together, no one was any worse off than anyone else. They all wore the same uniform, and shivered at nights in their beds. Someone in the dormitory always cried themselves to sleep. The rules were strict, the punishments harsh. They all had to eat every morsel of food put in front of them, Leroy said. But at least they never went hungry.

Some of the children teased him about being black, called him names, but he wasn't alone in that either. There were other black children there, and they learnt early on to turn a deaf ear and a blind eye to all that – it was the best way to deal with it, he told me, unless you wanted to get into fights all the time. He promised himself he'd get back at them in his own way, in his own time – and that's what he did too, as you'll see.

As a boy, Leroy was always top of the class, especially when it came to numbers and sums and mental arithmetic. But he was always talking in class when he shouldn't. One of his teachers started picking on him – he told me his name, but I've forgotten it – called him a troublemaker and was always standing him in the corner, 'where Darkies like him belonged', he'd say. Those were the very words he used. And this same teacher gave him the cane on his hand again and again for not trying hard enough.

"He wanted me to cry," Leroy said, "which is why I never did." After a while Leroy decided he wouldn't speak to him, wouldn't even say 'good morning, sir' with the others, when he came into the classroom. He got whacked again, for dumb insolence this time.

But one day, everything changed. Leroy won the school race on Sports Day. He beat everyone, including those twice his age and size. No one caned him again after that, and no one called

him 'Darky' again either. And then they found out he was a real wizard at football, that he could dribble and shoot the ball better than anyone they'd ever had at the school before. Season after season he won all the matches for them. He was given a new nickname, and one that he liked this time, 'The Wizard'.

And he wasn't only a wizard on the football pitch. He discovered there was something he could do even better than football. He could sing. If ever there was a solo to be sung in the choir, then Leroy was chosen to sing it. The best moment of his life when he was a boy was when the choir was invited to go and sing in St Paul's Cathedral, and he got up and sang 'Oh for the Wings of a Dove'. He told me that while he was singing, when he heard his voice soaring up high into that great dome, it was as if he really did have wings. Best feeling in the world, he said.

And he was right.

Whenever we could, we used to go on walks in the fields around Poperinge. And one day he began singing to me – 'Down by the Sally Gardens', it was. Then Leroy and I found ourselves dancing. Can you imagine? Out in the open, under blue skies, in a field in Flanders, dancing. For once the guns were silent. He had his arms around me, and he was humming 'Down by the Sally Gardens' softly in my ear. I never imagined I could be so happy, that anyone could be that happy.

Your Country Needs You

*B*ut I'm getting ahead of myself. I don't want to miss anything out.

By the time Leroy's voice broke, he was out of the orphanage, apprenticed to a carpenter, and playing football for his local side. Whenever he played, wherever he played, he was still 'The

Wizard'. The name stuck with him and stayed. The home supporters loved him, but when they played away the crowd would sometimes call him all manner of horrible things from the terraces. But that only made him play all the harder to win, to make them eat their words. He had found his way of getting back at them.

He had an offer to play for The Arsenal the week before war broke out, in August 1914 it was. In the newspapers they called him 'the wonder wizard of Walworth'. He'd soon be playing not just for The Arsenal, but for England too, they wrote. He was that good. But all his footballing pals were joining up, everyone in the team. There were posters all around, everywhere you looked: 'Your Country Needs You', 'For King and Country'.

Leroy was swept along on a tide of enthusiasm, patriotism, and optimism, as they all were, as I was too. The whole country was. He knew he had to go where and when his country called. It was his duty. Leroy stuck with his pals, his football team. They all joined up together, and went off across the Channel to fight. So Leroy never played for The Arsenal, nor for England either.

By the time I met him that day in the café in Poperinge only a few months later, seven of the football team who'd joined up with him were already dead.

"I'm the only forward left," Leroy told me. "But I can run faster than any of them, dodge and duck and dive – you should see me. No Fritz bullet's going to catch me, Martha girl," he said. "You'll see."

He told me he had to be back with his regiment in a couple of days. They'd be moving up again into the Front Line, into the trenches. "Tomorrow evening, same time, same place? To say goodbye?"

"I'll try," I said.

But we had a lot of casualties in from the Front that day, so it was late and nearly dark by the time I could get away. I had no leave pass this time, because I knew they wouldn't give me one if I asked, not two days in a row. So I skipped off without permission. I'd be back in an hour or so, no one would even know I'd been gone. That's what I told myself, that's what I hoped.

I knew he'd be waiting, however late I was. Jasper was lying at his feet looking very fed up. Leroy was the only one sitting there. I didn't have to be back on duty until six o'clock the next morning. All I knew, all he knew, was that we wanted to spend every moment we had left together. We forgot everything else. We found a little room above the café, with peeling flowery wallpaper and a narrow bed. We spent the whole night holding one another, loving one another. Jasper kept trying to jump up onto the bed, but we pushed him off. We wanted to be alone. Jasper didn't think much of that.

When I woke in the morning, Leroy was gone. It was already past seven o'clock. I knew I'd be in big trouble when I got back. I ran all the way just the same. In the end I got off quite lightly. They put me on report of course. After a dressing-down from the Major, who ticked me off in no uncertain terms about neglect of duty, he told me there were to be no more leave passes for me for two months. There were dire warnings too about what would happen to me if ever I went off like that again. But I didn't mind. I was on cloud nine, and that's where I stayed for the weeks that followed, until the morning I got to the hospital, and saw Jasper sitting outside, waiting.

I knew at once. One of the nurses told me. Joanna she was called, I remember – she was a lot older than the others and turned out to be the kindest of my friends. She warned me as I came in. But nothing and no one could prepare me for what I saw. Leroy was lying there unconscious, hands at his sides, hardly breathing, barely living. He'd been wounded

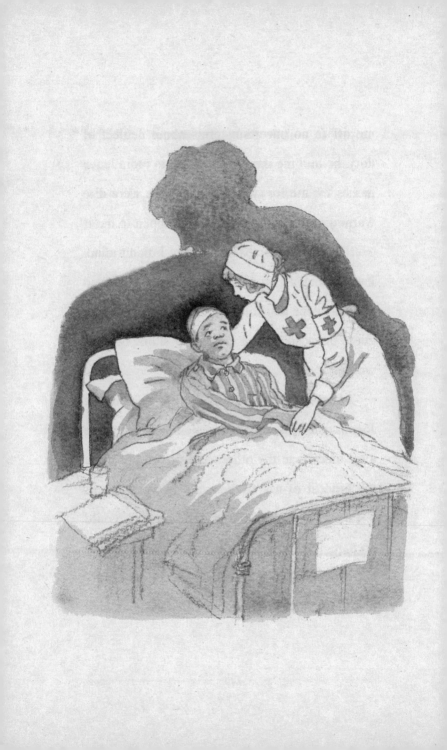

in his leg and in his back, I was told, and had lost a lot of blood. I was there beside him holding his hand when he woke up. He didn't know me, not at first.

I tried to go about my nursing duties as before, but it was hard for me to leave his bedside, especially when the infection set in and the fever made him delirious. I could tell from the look on the doctor's face that Leroy had very little chance. So many of them died of infection. All I could do with him, as I had with so many others, was to try to keep him cool, and make sure the dressings on his wound were changed often, and pray. I prayed so hard for him, begging God to let him live, promising I'd pray every day for the rest of my life, and go to church again every Sunday.

I sat all night and every night with him. This soldier was my soldier, and I was his sweetheart, his real sweetheart. Joanna tried to persuade me to let her sit in for me, told me I had to get some rest, to go to bed, but I wouldn't leave him. Sometimes I'd hum the songs he'd taught me, 'Sally Gardens' mostly, so he'd know I was still there. And Jasper stayed too, sitting outside on the hospital steps, just waiting. Doctors, nurses, and walking wounded would come by, and feed Jasper and talk to him. Everyone knew who he was waiting for by this time, just as everyone knew about Leroy and me. I was there at his bedside when he opened his eyes one morning and smiled up at me.

"Jasper all right?" he asked. I felt his forehead. The fever had gone.

Lucky Beggar

*W*e had a precious few weeks together in the hospital, as patient and nurse, but of course we were a lot more to one another than that. We didn't try to disguise it. There wasn't any point. Everyone knew. I didn't much care whether the nurses and doctors approved or not by now, and there were plenty around the hospital who tutted, I knew that. But all his pals who came to visit, sometimes half a dozen at a time, loved him like I did – well, not quite as much as I did perhaps. He seemed like a best friend to all of them.

They said what a 'lucky beggar' he was. Bobby did most of the talking when they came – he'd been the goalkeeper in the football team back home. He was the one who told me how it had happened, how when the whistle had gone, they'd gone over the top into No Man's Land, Leroy kicking a football ahead of him, Jasper running along beside him, as he always did. But they hadn't got far, about halfway across, before the German machine guns opened fire and the shells started falling all around. Several of them went down. They had to take shelter in a crater, in a shell hole, Jasper still with them. They lay there all day and into the night.

When it had all quietened down, they heard the sound of a man crying out for help, screaming in pain. Leroy didn't think twice about it, they told me. He clambered up out of the shell hole and went out there, out into No Man's Land, to fetch him back. But once he found him he discovered there were two more men lying out there as well, both badly wounded, one of them unconscious. Twice more he crawled out into No Man's Land to bring them back. And still no one spotted him. But the last time Leroy went out there, the flares went up and he was caught out in the open. Machine guns opened up, rifle fire.

That was when he was hit, shot in the leg.

Three lives he saved that day, and without a thought for his own. They were all on the way back across No Man's Land, carrying the wounded men with them when the shelling started and Leroy went down, hit again, a shrapnel wound this time. Bobby piggybacked him back to the trenches. "He was awful heavy to carry, I can tell you," he said.

It was from Bobby and his other pals that I learnt so much more about Leroy than he'd ever told me himself. He was just a Private soldier, the same rank they all were, but Leroy was the one they always followed. They believed he was lucky. Leroy and Jasper – they were like talismans to them, lucky mascots.

"All we've got out here is luck, luck and

pluck," Bobby told me one day after the visit was over, as we walked out of the hospital ward together. "Leroy's lucky. So we stay as close to him as we can. That way we get lucky too. He got a lucky wound, a Blighty one, so like as not they'll send him home. Never seen pluck like it, bringing those boys in like he did. He should get a ruddy Victoria Cross for that, if you ask me. It's what we all want, a medal for Leroy. We told the officers what he did, the whole story, that he deserves a medal. Course, being like he is, they probably won't give him one. But I'm telling you, there won't be no justice in this world if Leroy doesn't get a medal."

Bobby was wrong. They didn't send him home. Instead, they sent him to another hospital further behind the lines for rest and recuperation, and within a couple of months he was back in the trenches. And Bobby was right: there was no medal for Leroy either, but more about that later. Leroy wrote me a letter every day. Each of his letters was like a song to me. I could hear his voice in every word he wrote. I read them over and over last thing at night, and prayed to God to protect him. God is good, I kept telling myself. God is kind. God is listening. He'll look after my Leroy.

It was Bobby who came to the hospital a few weeks later, and told me how it happened, how Leroy had been killed. They were going forward up a hill to attack a German machine gun post, Leroy kicking the football ahead, leading the charge as usual, Jasper at his side, when they saw him fall.

Bobby said you always knew when a man was shot dead, killed outright – he'd seen it often. A dead body just crumples. Leroy collapsed and lay still. He didn't suffer, he assured me, just went out like a light. They tried to go out and bring him back, but the Germans counter-attacked, so they had to leave him where he was. They never saw him again. Jasper must have stayed with him or been killed. They never saw the dog again, either.

At first, when I became ill, the doctor at the hospital thought it must be out of grief, and gave me leave for a couple of days. I spent most of the time walking the fields around Poperinge, sitting in the café, remembering. When I got a fever, a few days later, they told me I'd caught an infection. The infection did pass, but it left me weakened and unable to carry out my duties. That's why they sent me home.

Mary, who knew everything from my letters – I'd hidden nothing from her – met me at the station in London and took me back by train to Scotland, and home to Aberdeenshire. I knew already that she didn't approve. But now I was home, now we were together, there were no recriminations, no blame, only kindness. Mary and Mother nursed me as best they could and Father prayed at my bedside and encouraged me to read the Bible more, to pray more. "It's the only way to find comfort," he told me. But I wouldn't pray, and I wouldn't read the Bible. Hadn't I prayed to this same God, his God, night after night out in Belgium, and hadn't he deserted me? He had not saved Leroy. And besides, no loving God I could imagine would have allowed such suffering as I had witnessed at the Front.

For weeks on end I lay there in bed, losing the will to live with every day that passed. The doctor was called in to see me. Dr Glennie. He was a peaky-looking man with cold hands, often with a dewdrop on his nose. One morning he came and examined me, listened to me, tapped me, and then peered at me severely over his spectacles.

"I know exactly what's wrong with you, my girl," he told me. "You'll be having a baby, in about six months' time." He also added, just for good measure, how upset my father would be, that I had brought shame upon my whole family, my church, the entire village. I hardly heard him. All I could think was that I would be having Leroy's baby, that Leroy was still with me, still alive within me. In that moment all my sorrow lifted. I had something to live for again.

I called him Roy

My father never spoke to me again. A few hours after the doctor left Mary came up to my room to tell me that Father had said I would have to leave the house as soon as I was well enough and never return. She had tried, Mother had tried, all they could to persuade him to relent, but he was adamant.

"So I told him straight," Mary said, "if Martha goes, I go."

These were my father's very words in reply, "Then go. I have no need of such faithless daughters."

I never forgot those words, as I have never forgotten Mary's goodness to me. I left everything to her, all the arrangements, where we would go when I was strong enough to travel, how we would live. Our greatest regret was that we had to leave our dear Mother behind. She promised she would come and visit when we were settled, which she did from time to time. But I never saw Father again, nor did Mary. All our lives, Mother did all she could to bring us together, to forge some kind of reconciliation, but he remained implacable until the day he died.

Mary took me far away, to a place where no one knew us, to a little cottage outside a seaside village in Cornwall – near Penzance it was – because she thought the sea air would be healthy for a growing child. Here I had my baby. I called him Roy, and he was as handsome as his father had been, and so like him in every way – how he looked at me, how he laughed. Even as a baby he already had his father's big hands.

I think we would have stayed in Cornwall all our lives if we'd had a choice; we loved it there. Mary was teaching at the local school, I was nursing the baby, who was growing up healthy and strong. We'd sit on the sand in the sunshine and watch the fishing boats coming in and out of the harbour. The war, still going on across the sea, seemed a whole world away. But tongues were wagging in the village.

It was common enough everywhere in those days for a mother to be left alone with fatherless children. There were several families like that in the village. After all, hundreds of thousands of young fathers had been killed out there. But Leroy had been black.

Roy was much less obviously black than his father, but still noticeably darker than anyone else in the village, and darker than me too. Some people wouldn't speak to us. Some even crossed the village street to avoid us. Most weren't like that of course, but there were enough disapproving glances, enough tittle-tattle to cast a long shadow over our lives. We were beginning to feel like outcasts.

Then one morning, our landlord – the local farmer – came to the door and told us we'd have to leave. He didn't say why, but we knew the reason. We had two weeks to pack up and go, he said. "We don't want your sort around here," he said, "and what's more we don't want your kind teaching our children."

Mary was at once incandescent with rage, and told the farmer just what she thought of him, and then drove him out of the cottage with a broom. It was quite a spectacle!

Mary decided we had to move away, as soon as possible, as far away as possible from these 'miserable people' as she called them. It was a newspaper report that gave her the idea. There'd been another Zeppelin air raid on London and lots of people had been killed and wounded. I remember she sat me down at the kitchen table as I was feeding Roy, and told me she'd worked it all out.

"Wherever we go we can be sure it will be the same," she said. "They'll look at you and little Roy and they'll gossip away, they'll weave their wicked tales. Well I'm not having it. I'm not. So I've decided we must invent a story of our own, about us. Now, this Zeppelin raid on London – there will be orphans, won't there? There are bound to be orphans. We shall adopt one of them. His father will have come from Barbados and has been killed in Belgium – truth in that – and his mother will be from London, killed in this Zeppelin raid. We will be the sisters of that mother, and being the nearest relatives, his aunties, her only family, we will look after the baby. The natural thing to do. Must happen all the time. That will be our story, little Roy's story. We won't live too close to London – don't want to be near those Zeppelins when they come over, do we? I've read about seaside places in Kent, seen pictures too. I like the look of Folkestone, it's a lovely town. Roy will still grow up by the sea, and no one will know us. And when they ask, as they will, we'll just tell them our story. Simple. We shall find a place to live. There are schools in Folkestone. I shall teach. All will be well, Martha. Don't you worry."

We'll tell him later

So that's what we did, moved to the other end of the country and if anyone asked who little Roy was, we told them the Zeppelin story. And that's where Roy grew up, by the sea in Folkestone. I stayed home and looked after him and the house and the garden, and Mary was a teacher in a junior school nearby – she became a headteacher in the end. A wonderful teacher she was too. It's true she could be a bit sharp, a bit brusque, with the children, but she was always kindhearted towards them. She had their best interests at heart, and they knew it.

Of course it all turned out to be a lot more complicated than either Mary or I had first imagined. What we hadn't realised at first was that we'd have to live out our story, not simply tell it. And for Roy that story was the story of who he was, how he came to be with us. Roy grew up not just calling me 'Auntie', but believing that's what I was to him. When he asked about himself, as of course he often did when he grew old enough, we'd tell him about the Zeppelin raid, about how his mother, our sister, had been killed in it, and how his father had died in Belgium in the war – that bit was much easier to talk about than the rest, I can tell you.

We told him how as a little baby he had survived the Zeppelin raid and been brought out alive from the ruins of the house. Every day as he grew up I yearned to tell him the truth, that I was his mother. I wanted him to know all about Leroy, and about Jasper. I longed for him to call me Mummy, especially at the school gates when I saw and heard all the other children with their mothers. But Auntie Martha I was to him, and Auntie Martha I stayed. It was hard to bear, but I knew it had to be. I locked the secret in my heart and kept it there.

In a way, Jasper was Roy's idea. He loved

dogs and was always asking if we could have one. My little boy, once he got an idea into his head he'd never let it go. Mary always said no. I never argued with her. I knew better than that. I just did it. Without telling her, I went and bought Roy a dog for his tenth birthday. I found one just like his father had had in the trenches, like the one I'd met at the café that day in Poperinge, a little white Jack Russell with black eyes. When I brought the dog home, Roy wasn't back from school. I told Mary we had to call him Jasper. As it turned out she didn't object at all. It was unspoken, but she knew fine why I had to call him Jasper, why I'd chosen a little white Jack Russell terrier, that Jasper and Leroy were lying out there somewhere in a field in Belgium, undiscovered; that I thought of them every day of my life.

When Roy came back from school that day he was ecstatic. He said we were 'the best, the most supreme aunties in the whole wide world'. Jasper instantly became one of the family, and Roy's favourite playmate, always game for a game, if you know what I mean. And always there to comfort Roy when he was sad – Jasper seemed to have an instinct for that. Like any good friend, he knew when he was needed most. They were inseparable.

Roy grew up to be so like his father. He had the same open face and easy smile that had first enchanted me, and like his father, he turned out to be a wizard with a football, and he could sing quite wonderfully too. Like his father he was pretty good with sums as well, 'bright as a button' his teacher told me at mental arithmetic. I taught him the songs his father had taught me, and I always asked him to sing the same song for me on my birthday, as a special treat: 'Down by the Sally Gardens'. I only had to close my eyes and it was Leroy's voice, Leroy singing, Leroy humming.

If you tell a story often enough – no, let's be honest, let's call it what it was, a lie – if you tell a lie often enough, and for long enough, particularly if you live it, in the end you forget it's a story altogether, you forget it's a lie. You come to believe it, and I suppose that's what happened. In time, I no longer even noticed when Roy called me Auntie Martha. As he grew up, Mary and I endlessly talked over whether or not the time had come now to tell Roy the truth at last. But our secret had been lived out for too long. Neither of us wanted to risk telling him, Mary least of all. She always said that we should die taking the secret with us.

"'What the mind doesn't know, the heart can't grieve over.' Let's just leave it alone," she'd say, "at least wait till he's twenty-one. We'll tell him then." So we left it alone and never told him. We shouldn't have done, but we did. We left it too late.

Roy was just nineteen when the Second World War began in September 1939. He joined up at once as so many young men did, and was soon a pilot in the RAF. He was out in France with his squadron when he met this French girl. He wrote us long letters about her. Both of them got out of France just in

"The Aces" of the Royal Air Force co-operating with the Russian Air Force.

BACK THEM UP!

time, just before the fall of Dunkirk. He brought her to see us. Christine she was called. You call her Maman. He was very proud of her, so very fond of her, and once we'd got to know her so were we, and so was Jasper.

The wedding soon after was a quiet affair,

in a Registry Office in Folkestone – just Mary, me, the two of them – and Jasper. Roy insisted that Jasper had to be there. I remember he had a bit of an argument with the man in the Registry Office about that, but Roy was in his Flight Lieutenant's RAF uniform. He was a Spitfire pilot, and he looked like it, and that helped, helped a lot. Jasper was allowed in, and sat beside me all the way through the wedding. Actually, he slept through most of it.

We were living through the Battle of Britain that summer of 1940. The skies above us were the battlefield. We'd see the German fighters and bombers coming over in their hundreds, watched the dogfights, hoped and prayed every day that Roy was all right.

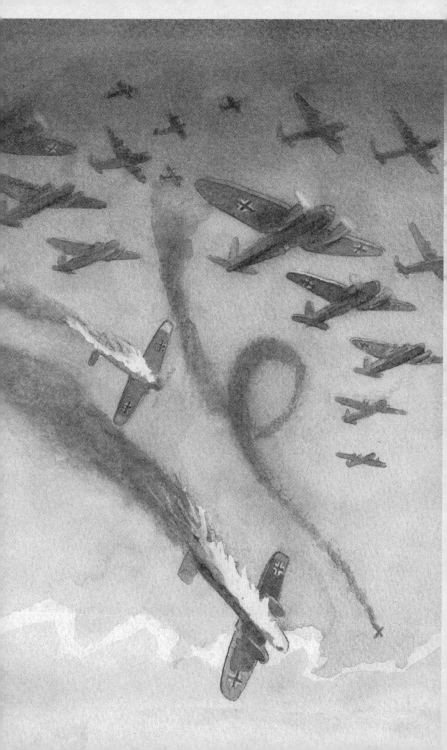

He was stationed not far away at RAF Manston; so for a while Christine came to live with us here in his old room, and worked as a waitress in the town. When the phone rang that day in September 1940, I answered it. The call was from Manston. It was Roy's Wing Commander. He asked if I was Roy's wife. I said that Roy's wife lived with us, but that she wasn't in.

"Are you his mother then?" he asked.

I shouldn't have said it, but I did. "Yes," I told him.

"Then perhaps you could break the news, perhaps you could tell his wife... be better coming from you perhaps."

"Tell her what?" I said.

"That Roy was killed this morning. We don't

know exactly what happened yet. An engine failure on his Spitfire, we think, on take-off it was. He crashed. I am so sorry. He was a fine man, and a brave flying officer, the bravest of the brave. Everyone here thought the world of him here. We shall miss him more than we can say."

A Happier Place

Mary and I, we told your Maman together when she came home from work that evening, told her as gently as we could. She sat there unable to speak, unable even to cry. We made her cocoa and put her to bed. She lay curled up on her bed for about a week, refusing all the food we offered her. She just lay there, rocking herself. There was no comforting her. I came in to see her one morning and she was sitting up looking out to sea, with Jasper beside her on the bed – he'd hardly left her side the whole time. Jasper might have been old and slow by now, but he still knew where he was most needed.

"I don't want Roy to have been burnt, to have died in flames," she said, without turning round. "I want him to have gone down out there, out at sea. Is that how it happened? Tell me that's how it happened."

"Yes," I told her. "Out in the Channel it was."

I told Mary what she'd said, and she agreed that it could only hurt her more if Christine knew the truth about how he had been killed. Ever since we heard the news about Roy I had longed to tell her the whole truth about Leroy, to put my arms around her and tell her that I was Roy's mother, to share my grief, share hers. I couldn't do it even then, but as I sat beside her, I did say that I had lost a dear, dear friend in the First World War, and had never forgotten him. And I did say that Roy may have been our adopted son, but that we had never thought of him as that. To us, I said, he had always been simply our son, and always would be. It was a kind of truth, at least.

Well, Michael, the rest you know, or can guess. Like me, all those years before, your Maman discovered she would be having a baby. We wanted her to stay on and live with us. We begged her not to go to London where the bombing was inflicting such terrible damage, but despite all that, despite all we said, she was determined to go. There was translation and interpreting work she could do there, for the war effort, she said. She had to go, had to do it. She explained that it was because she was French, because her country was occupied by the enemy, and because that enemy had killed the man she loved. She promised she would come down to see us as often as she could. And she always has.

So you were born in London, Michael, and I had a grandson. You had a grandmother and never knew it. Now you do. Now you know everything. Look after the photo of your father, polish the frame for me, and tell your children my story, because it's your story and theirs. Look after Auntie Pish for me, won't you, as she looked after me. And go and see the place where your grandfather lies, out in Belgium – I never had the courage to do that. He would like that. I would too. We'll be together again by then, Leroy and I, in a happier place, a peaceful place, where the colour of a man's skin is invisible, where no lies are told, because none are needed, where all is well.

I send you all my love,

Your grandmother

(And your Auntie Snowdrop!)

Secret Lives

I FINISHED READING AND SAT THERE FOR A LONG while, simply trying to take it all in, to piece together this new family I had just acquired, to picture my grandfather, to take on board what all this meant. Auntie Snowdrop had just redrawn the map of my life, and had become my grandmother. I had a grandfather and a past I'd never known about. All this was difficult enough to get my head around. But Auntie Snowdrop had left me with a dilemma. She had confided in me the deepest secrets of her life, and I didn't know what to do with them.

Any moment now I'd hear the front door open, and Jasper would be charging up the stairs and barging open my door, and Maman would be calling for me. I knew what the choice was: either I could hide away the writing pad and keep Auntie Snowdrop's secret locked inside me forever, or I could tell Maman. I picked up the photo of Papa, and looked into his eyes, into his heart, hoping he might tell me somehow what to do. He did.

All his life, he hadn't known who his own father and mother were, what wonderful and brave people they were. I knew how much he would love to have known. The more I thought about it, the more I knew I would tell Maman, that I had to, that I wanted to. I remembered then how I'd pestered her all those years before when I was little to tell me more about Papa, how angry I'd been when she wouldn't tell me. Well, how could she have told me? She didn't even know. And I was about to tell her. In time I would tell everyone – I wanted to shout it out. Auntie Snowdrop had been right: now that I knew who I was, I was proud of it. I wanted the world to know. I was from Barbados, from Scotland and from France. How rare was that! How special was that! I couldn't wait for Maman to come back, to tell her everything.

I was downstairs in the kitchen, waiting for her. I heard the key in the door.

"Cooee!" she called. "I'm back." I sat there not saying a word as she put the kettle on. Then I told her I had got something to tell her, and that it was very important, that she had to sit down. She looked worried. "What is it, *chéri*?" she asked. "Is something wrong?" Jasper hopped into his basket and listened, ears pricked, as if he knew what I was about to do, as if he knew perfectly well the story I was about to tell was important for him too, that he was part of it, as of course he was, in a way.

"Maman," I began. I opened Auntie Snowdrop's writing pad in front of me on the table. "I've got things I have to tell you, about me, about you, about Auntie Snowdrop, Papa, everyone. You see this writing pad? Well, Jasper knocked over the photo of Papa and the glass broke, and I found it hidden in the back, behind the photograph. I was meant to find it. Auntie Snowdrop told me where to look for it years ago, but I didn't understand. It's like a kind of a letter-story, from Auntie Snowdrop to me. I'm going to read it to you out loud."

"What's it about?" Maman asked, sitting down.

"Secret lives," I told her.

She sat very upright in her chair, and tense, one hand holding the other, her fingers twiddling her wedding ring. She seemed to be preparing herself. I began to read.

As I read, I'd look up at her from time to time trying to guess her thoughts, as all the family secrets and myths unfolded. Throughout, Maman sat there, almost expressionless, swallowing sometimes as she tried to control her tears, still twiddling her ring. I could hear Auntie Snowdrop's voice in the telling, hear her voice in mine.

After it was over Maman said nothing for a while. Then she turned to me and hugged me so tight, I thought she would never let go. Then, holding me at arm's length, she said: "Your Papa would so love to have known all that. To know he had a father like Leroy would have meant so much to him. She should have told him, told him everything. He had a right to know. And she should have told me too."

"Did you mind hearing the truth about how Papa was killed?" I asked.

She smiled at me then. "Strangely enough, that's about the only part of the story I did know," she said. "A couple of months after he died, when I felt I could face it, I went to Manston, to the RAF air station, to meet his Wing Commander, to find out more, to collect your father's things, his clothes, his medals, his photos and so on. The officer told me then that he had crashed on take-off. I never blamed the Aunties for not telling me, and certainly not now I know who Auntie Snowdrop really was. And after all, she was only telling me what I suppose I wanted to hear – that he had crashed into the sea, died a hero's death, fighting in the skies."

"So you knew," I said, even now feeling slightly resentful that she had kept this from me. "Every time when we went down there to Folkestone you knew he wasn't out there in the Channel. When we spread the snowdrops on the sea to remember him, you knew."

"Yes," Maman told me. "But I also knew that Auntie Snowdrop wanted me to go on believing their story, and I suppose I wanted to believe it too, even though I already knew the truth. The truth is sometimes so hard to accept. But I can accept it now, all of it. In the end you have to, don't you?" She looked up at me then, with a smile. "You should do it one day, *mon petit chou*," she went on, "do what Auntie Snowdrop says."

"What?" I asked.

"Go to Belgium. Go to the battlefield where your grandfather was killed, where he still lies. You should go."

June 2, 2012

I didn't go, not for years, not for decades. To be honest I think I just forgot about it. Life overtakes us. I was busy for years growing up, being a father and then a grandfather myself. And then, maybe it was just old age – I'm nearly seventy now after all. Are these reasons or excuses for delaying as long as I did? I don't know.

Auntie Pish lived on well into her nineties. She mellowed, and became in her later years as sweet as her sister had been. I did just as Auntie Snowdrop had asked me to, and never told Auntie Pish about any of it.

Maman died only last year, also in her nineties. We live a long time in my family, unless wars take us young. It was while I was sorting through some family things after she died, rummaging through suitcases and cardboard boxes full of half-forgotten memories, that I came across one of Papa's medals again – it was the one I'd had as a child, with the blue ribbon. That was what prompted me to search out Auntie Snowdrop's story again – even after all these years I could never get used to thinking of her as Grandma however hard I tried.

I read it again out loud to my family the Christmas before last, when they all came down to see me. *Their story too*, I thought, and they should know it. After I'd finished, one of my grandchildren, the oldest at fourteen – she'd been called Christine after my mother – said how wrong and unfair it was that Great Great Grandfather Leroy had never got a medal for his bravery in the First World War. "It was just because he was black, wasn't it?" she said. That decided me.

Christine and I would start a campaign to see if we could put it right. I did my research in the Imperial War Museum, sifted through dozens of regimental records. The more I looked into it the more I could see that an injustice had been done, that Leroy's bravery had been overlooked. Deliberate or not? Who knows? Then Christine and I sat down and between us wrote to everyone we could think of, the Prime Minister, the Queen, the Minister of Defence. But it was hopeless. Some didn't even reply, most just palmed us off. It was too long after the event, they all said. To review a case like this they needed new evidence and there was no new evidence. We did a couple of radio programmes, but nothing came of it.

It was Christine's idea, a couple of years later, to go to Belgium, to see where her Great Great Grandfather Leroy had died, to put things right our own way. We went. We found his name carved on the Menin Gate, in Ypres, amongst the 50,000 and more other soldiers with no known graves. We visited the Flanders Field Museum and bought a map of the battlefield, saw exactly the field where he died, the hill he must have charged up that day with his pals, with Jasper. There was a farm nearby, at the top of the hill. We had the car with us, and Jasper – not the same Jasper of course, but a white Jack Russell terrier with black eyes like all the others the family has had down the years. It's a family tradition I've kept going all my life – I've had five Jaspers in all now. You could say this whole story was about Jasper, in a way.

Christine did the map-reading. We found the farm, and parked in the farmyard. Jasper had run on ahead of us up towards the wood at the top of the field, chasing after some crows. Christine checked the map. She was sure this had to be the place, here or hereabouts anyway, closer to the wood, she thought. We followed Jasper. It was peaceful farmland now, a tractor making hay up on the ridge, cows grazing contentedly in a field nearby, and a church bell ringing in the distance. Jasper was snuffling about under a fallen tree at the edge of the wood.

"Wherever Jasper stops, if he ever does, wherever he next sits down for a rest. That's where we'll do it," I said. "Agreed?"

"Agreed, Grandpa," Christine replied.

Jasper had finished his snuffling by now, and was exploring along the tree line on the crest of the hill, nose to the ground. We followed. After a while he looked back at us, stopped, sat down and waited for us to come up the hill to join him.

"Here then," said Christine. "Right here."

So that's where we dug the hole. Christine laid Papa's medal in the earth. "The medal they never gave you, Great Great Grandfather," she said. "We're giving it to you now, because you deserve it. It was your son's, my great grandfather's, and now it's yours too. You can share it."

We pushed the earth back over the medal, trod in the turf, and stood there quietly for a few moments, each of us alone in our thoughts. That's when Christine reminded me about the envelope I'd brought with me. I'd forgotten all about it. She did it for me, crouching down to scatter them on the grass, all the pressed snowdrops from my diary, every one that Auntie Snowdrop had given me all those years before.

"From Martha," Christine whispered.

"From Auntie Snowdrop," I said.

Some floated away on the breeze, almost at once, as light and as insubstantial as gossamer, but a few stayed clinging to the grass at our feet, enough to mark the place.

After a while we walked away. But Jasper sat there on the spot for some time, before he came running after us.

Afterwards we went to Poperinge and sat in a café with Jasper at our feet. I don't know if it was the right café, and it doesn't matter. We had egg and chips, and I had a cold white Belgian beer. Christine gave most of her chips to Jasper. From the look on his face he thought they were the best chips in the whole wide world.

POSTSCRIPT

It was a phone call from Michael Foreman that set me thinking about writing this book. Had I read or heard about Lieutenant Walter Tull, he asked me, the only black officer to serve in the British Army in the First World War? I hadn't. But I did my research, and discovered how this extraordinary young man had grown up in an orphanage in London, had played football for Spurs, then joined up with his pals when the war began in 1914. As a soldier he was much respected, and brave beyond belief, his actions on the field of battle worthy of a medal for gallantry. He never received one. He died leading his men in attack in 1918. He has no known grave.

Walter Tull's life was the inspiration for Leroy in my story. I have not attempted to portray the actual Walter Tull in *A Medal for Leroy*, but you will find many of the aspects of his life incorporated into my character Leroy. And many of the themes in the book, and the issues raised, spring from the life and death of this brave young man. This is why the book is dedicated to his memory.

A story is much like a river. My river in this book is the life of Leroy, and his family. But many smaller autobiographical streams flow into it. I did have two aunties, Auntie Bess and Auntie Julie with whom I grew up, who were inseparable. My Uncle Pieter was killed in the RAF in 1940, as a young man of twenty-one, and only recently were the true circumstances of his death unearthed. Many families, including mine, live with unspoken, often deliberately hidden secrets, as happens in this story. And I think it's true that many of us, certainly me, are fascinated to discover more about the lives of our parents and grandparents and even our great grandparents, because like it or not they make us who we are.

Michael Morpurgo

AFTERWORD

Walter Tull died in March 1918, one of over 400,000 soldiers killed or wounded in the sixteen-day-long Battle of the Somme. Like so many killed in the First World War, his body was never recovered and lies in a field somewhere in France; instead of a grave, Walter Tull's name is listed with more than 34,000 others on the Arras Memorial in France.

He was an exceptional soldier. His grandmother had been born a slave in the Caribbean, and his Barbadian father and English mother died when he was still a boy. He grew up in an orphanage in London yet went on to become the first black player at Tottenham Hotspur and Northampton Town – and the third ever black professional football player in the UK. British football fans were unused to seeing black players in those days, and sometimes shouted racist abuse at Tull.

When war broke out in 1914, the British Army unofficially rejected many black applicants by saying they failed their medical exam. But it was impossible to reject a footballer for being unfit, so Tull joined his colleagues in the 'Footballers' Battalion' and was promoted three times before reaching the battlefield.

At this time the Army rules stated that officers (those in authority) must be of 'pure European descent' and that black soldiers could hold an 'honorary rank' but not 'exercise any actual command or power'. However, Tull's excellent conduct in his first battle at the Somme, where only 79 of his regiment of 400 soldiers survived, impressed his superior so much he recommended Tull train to be an officer.

Despite official Army law, in May 1917 Tull became the first black combat officer in the British Army.

He led a successful night attack over the River Piave in Italy, and all of his soldiers returned safely, even though they were under heavy fire. His Commanding Officer praised his gallantry and coolness and recommended him for a Military Cross (a medal for junior officers who show gallantry fighting the enemy).

But Tull was never given the award. The Ministry of Defence does not hold the recommendation and we don't know why he was overlooked. Even though Tull didn't get the recognition he deserved, being commissioned as a black officer was exceptional for the time.

Two doctors from the West Indies applied to join the Royal Army Medical Corps but the War Office rejected them, in spite of their solid reputations, because they were not of 'pure European descent'.

The situation was not much better for black American soldiers in the First World War. Before the USA joined the war, a number of American men had volunteered to fight. One group was the Lafayette Flying Corps – American pilots who fought for France. When America joined the war in 1917, any

American volunteers were transferred to the US Army. On transfer, Eugene Bullard – the world's first black military pilot – who had flown in around twenty combat missions, was forbidden to fly for the US Army. He served the rest of the war as a foot soldier.

One black American soldier's recognition came posthumously. Like Tull, Freddie Stowers was also the grandson of a slave, showed heroism and gallantry, and died in battle in 1918. He was recommended for a Medal of Honor – the highest American military decoration – shortly after his death but the recommendation 'somehow got misplaced'. After an Army review, in 1991 President Bush presented Stowers' Medal of Honor to his surviving sisters.

Today, black American and British soldiers are no longer denied the honours they earn. In 2005 Johnson Beharry, a Grenadian soldier in the British Army, was the first living soldier since 1969 to receive the Victoria Cross – the highest British military decoration. The award recognised his

Walter Tull

Johnson Beharry

'extreme gallantry and unquestioned valour' when he drove his crew to safety from an ambush in Iraq while seriously injured.

And some effort is being made to right past wrongs. In 2006 a Maori sergeant was posthumously given the Victoria Cross, sixty-three years after his recommendation was 'inexplicably' revoked by a government official during the Second World War.

MICHAEL MORPURGO OBE is one of Britain's best-loved writers for children. He has written over 100 books and won many prizes, including the Smarties Prize, the Blue Peter Book Award and the Whitbread Award. His recent bestselling novels include *Shadow, An Elephant in the Garden* and *Born to Run*.

Michael's stories have been adapted numerous times for stage and screen, and he was Children's Laureate from 2003 to 2005, a role which took him all over the country to inspire children with the joy of reading stories.

Other titles by Michael Morpurgo include:

Little Manfred
Shadow
An Elephant in the Garden
Running Wild
Kaspar
Born to Run
The Amazing Story of Adolphus Tips
Farm Boy
The Butterfly Lion
Sparrow – the story of Joan of Arc
Outlaw – the story of Robin Hood